TiMe ^out FoR MoNSTeRS!

by Jean Reidy

Pictures by Robert Neubecker

DiSNEP · HYPERION BOOKS
NEW YORK

To Pat, Tim, Catherine, and Molly
 —J. R.

To my dad, and drawing in time out . . .
 —R. N.

Text copyright © 2012 by Jean Reidy
Illustrations copyright © 2012 by Robert Neubecker

First Edition
10 9 8 7 6 5 4 3 2 1
F850-6835-5-12105
Printed in Singapore

Library of Congress Cataloging-in-Publication Data
Reidy, Jean.
  Time out for monsters! / by Jean Reidy ; illustrations by Robert
Neubecker. —1st ed.
     p. cm.
  Summary: A little boy turns his "time out" into an adventure.
  ISBN 978-1-4231-3127-4
  [1. Imagination—Fiction. 2. Behavior—Fiction.] I. Neubecker, Robert,
ill. II. Title.
  PZ7.R273773Ti 2012
  [E]—dc22   2011013049

Reinforced binding
Art created using brush and India ink on Arches watercolor paper.
Color was applied digitally on a Mac.

Visit www.disneyhyperionbooks.com

THERE'S A CORNER IN MY HOUSE THAT NEEDS SOME FIXING UP....

MOM SAYS IT'S FINE,
BUT I KNOW BETTER.
I SPEND A **LOT** OF TIME
THERE.

YEAH, DEFINITELY SOME **COLOR**! AND A **WINDOW** SO I CAN SEE THE **YARD...**

AND A DUMP TRUCK

THIS CORNER NEEDS A COMFY SEAT WITH SOME PILLOWS...

FOR A KING!

AND THE KING NEEDS A DRAGON! A REALLY BIG DRAGON!

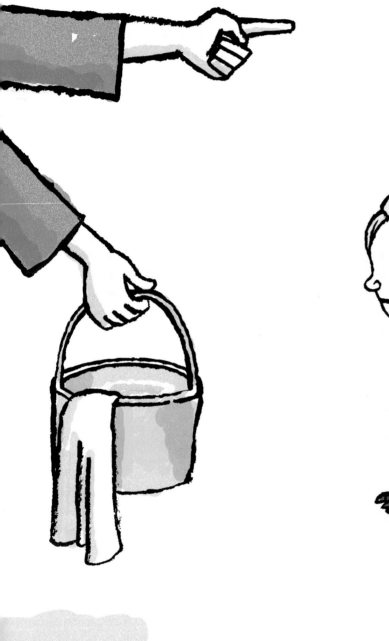